Owen
AND
Eleanor
Move In

Book 1

Written by H.M. Bouwman • Illustrated by Charlie Alder

First edition published 2018
Printed in the United States of America
25 24 23 22 21 20 19 18   1 2 3 4 5 6 7 8

Paperback ISBN: 9781506439723
Hardcover ISBN: 9781506449364
Ebook ISBN: 9781506439747

Written by H.M. Bouwman
Illustrated by Charlie Alder
Designed by 1517 Media

Library of Congress Cataloging-in-Publication Data

Names: Bouwman, H. M., author. | Alder, Charlie, illustrator.
Title: Owen and Eleanor move in / by H.M. Bouwman ; illustrated by Charlie
    Alder.
Description: First edition. | Minneapolis, MN : Sparkhouse Family, 2018. |
    Summary: Eight-year-old Eleanor is very unhappy when her family moves into
    a duplex, so she asks her new neighbor, seven-year-old Owen, to help her
    escape to her old house.
Identifiers: LCCN 2017037049 (print) | LCCN 2017049466 (ebook) | ISBN
    9781506439747 (Ebook) | ISBN 9781506439723 (pbk. : alk. paper)
Subjects: | CYAC: Homesickness--Fiction. | Moving, Household--Fiction. |
    Friendship--Fiction. | Family life--Fiction.
Classification: LCC PZ7.B6713 (ebook) | LCC PZ7.B6713 Owe 2018 (print) | DDC
    [Fic]--dc23
LC record available at https://lccn.loc.gov/2017037049

V81163; 9781506439723; JAN2018

Sparkhouse Family
510 Marquette Avenue
Minneapolis, MN 55402
sparkhousefamily.org

Chapter 1
Eleanor

To begin with, Scrumpy the Fourth went belly-up somewhere between the old house and the new house.

And Scrumpy the Fourth was almost brand-new, because Scrumpy the Third had keeled over only last week. "You poor little thing," Eleanor said to the dead goldfish. She tugged against her seat belt to curl over the fishbowl on her lap. "You kicked the bucket, you bought the farm, you bit the dust, you crushed up your chips—"

"That's not right," said Eleanor's older sister from the front seat. Alicia was in sixth grade and knew *everything*. *"Crush up your chips is wrong."*

"It is *not* wrong," said Eleanor. "If you crush up your chips, then your chips are dead." Alicia couldn't really argue with that. Crushed chips were no good, unless they were on top of corn-and-bean hot dish.

The car stopped. Eleanor climbed out. "See?" she said to her mom, who had been driving. "Scrumpy's a goner. That's *another* reason why we shouldn't move."

Eleanor's mother sighed.

Eleanor's dad stood in the doorway to the new duplex, next to her big brother Aaron, who was in high school. They were the same height, but Aaron was skinnier.

Dad said, "Come in! We've already put the beds together."

Mom and Alicia took bags of clothes from the trunk and walked up the steps into the new apartment. Eleanor marched slowly and majestically along the sidewalk, carrying her fishbowl and humming the tune from *Star Wars*. The old, old *Star Wars*. The one with Princess Leia. Eleanor was glad to be wearing her glitteriest skirt. Dead Scrumpy the Fourth deserved some honor.

Alicia and Mom went into the house with Aaron. Dad came down the steps toward Eleanor. "I'm sorry, honey. Will there be a funeral tonight?"

Eleanor stopped humming because she had suddenly thought of something. "We can't do a funeral here. It needs to be at the old house, in the backyard. With Scrumpy One, Two, and Three."

Dad said, "We don't own the old house anymore. This is our house now."

"Our *duplex*," said Eleanor. "And not even *ours*." She studied the two-family house. It was yellow. Their old house was blue. Eleanor hated yellow. She loved blue. She hated duplexes. She loved houses. Houses stood all by themselves with no one living above you. Houses were where you didn't have to be quiet and worry about waking someone up when you played superhero.

She'd already been warned about superhero.

Houses were places where you could nail gears and pulleys to your wall and no landlord got mad at you (except maybe Mom and Dad). She'd been warned about nails and pulleys too.

Houses might have a bedroom just for you, on the second floor. In a duplex, everyone was on the first floor because some other family was on the second floor, and you shared a room with your sister Alicia, who thought you were a baby because you were eight. Like Alicia had never been eight.

Eleanor thought a lot of things, but most of them were about how she didn't want to live here.

"Eleanor?" said Dad. "I really think you'll like the house."

"The *duplex*," said Eleanor.

"Fine. Yes." Dad walked toward the house, then turned back to her. "There's a boy living upstairs who is almost the same age as you. He's seven."

"I'm eight." Seven was not even close to the same as eight.

"Maybe you can be friends." He sighed. "People are flexible, Eleanor. You can adjust.

You can even learn to love a new home."

Eleanor turned and paraded down the sidewalk. This time she hummed the Darth Vader tune, in a very somber way. By the time she turned back, her dad had gone inside.

They don't care, she thought, *about the old house or the old neighborhood, and they don't care about Scrumpy the Fourth or about me. There will be a funeral—at the old house.* She held the goldfish bowl aloft, like Darth Vader might hold a lightsaber (except she had to use two hands because she didn't want to spill), and she tried to make her voice deep like Vader's. "I swear to you, Scrumpy the Fourth, that I will bring you back to your rightful home and bury you beside your family." *And,* she added to herself, *I'll move back there. Because I'm not staying here.* She buzzed the laser sound to make it all official.

"That's not how you hold a sword," said a high, light voice.

Eleanor looked. Almost hidden under the big pine tree on the edge of the yard, a small boy sat cross-legged. He had light-brown hair and glasses. Probably the seven-year-old. Probably only a first-grader.

The boy said, "I mean, if that's supposed to be a sword, you're doing it wrong."

Chapter 2
Owen

As soon as Owen said, "You're doing it wrong," he realized it was probably not the right thing to say to someone he was just meeting for the first time. Maybe it was even rude.

The girl, taller than him with black curly hair and dark-brown eyes—and lots of glittery pink stuff everywhere else—seemed to think he *was* rude. She huffed. "It's not a sword. It's a lightsaber." She held the goldfish bowl higher, and the water sloshed, the fish floating at the top like it was sleeping. "I'm training to be a Jedi, so I know how to hold a lightsaber. This is exactly how."

"Um . . . okay," said Owen.

"Anyway, are you only seven?" asked the girl, glaring at him like it was a really important question.

"I'm not *only* seven." Owen's little brother was *only five*. "I'm *already* seven." There was a huge difference between *only* and *already*.

"Huh. Are you going into *second grade*?" She said it like it was a bad thing.

Owen could never remember what grade he was in. But luckily, just then his mom came outside, carrying a plate. "Mom, am I going into first grade, or second grade?"

She frowned, thinking. "I think by now you're a second-grader." Then she turned to the girl. "You must be our downstairs neighbor. I'm Kathleen."

"I'm not allowed to call grown-ups by first names," said the girl. "And how can you not know what grade your kid is in? Is he . . . ?" She paused. "Is he someone you just adopted yesterday, and you don't know if he can read, so you don't know what grade he should go into? Or maybe he's been really, really sick for years and years"—she squinted at him—"or months and months, and he's missed a ton of school, and you don't know if he can keep going in his same grade or not? Or maybe . . ."

"I'm homeschooled," said Owen.

"And we don't think about grades that much," said his mom.

The girl looked disappointed. "Are you sure you weren't maybe kidnapped by a secret society and you just escaped and now you have to start school, later than everyone else, and they don't know if you can catch up because all you've learned is how to talk in secret code and be a spy?"

"Pretty sure," said Owen.

"I'll leave you two," said Mom. "Owen, I'm going to introduce myself to . . . what's your name?"

"Eleanor," said the girl.

"I'm going to say hi to Eleanor's mom."

"My mom went to the store for toilet paper

because we can't find any in the unpacking. Dad's home."

"Well, I'll drop this off with your dad then." She left with her plate, but this time to the lower duplex, where she knocked and chatted with Eleanor's dad before heading upstairs again.

The girl (Eleanor) still looked disappointed about the homeschooling.

"I wasn't kidnapped," said Owen, "but I do know secret codes. And I take fencing lessons. You know, with swords. I can teach you about sword fighting."

"This is a *lightsaber*." Then she shrugged and put down the bowl on the sidewalk. "It's not even the right shape for a lightsaber. Pretty pathetic, really."

Owen peered in. The fish did not look good. "Is he . . . dead?"

"Dead as crushed-up chips," Eleanor said cheerily. "Which means yes. We're going to have a funeral. You're invited."

"Oh. I mean, thank you." Owen had only been to one funeral before, and that was when he was too little to remember. "I won't have to give a speech, will I?" He didn't like giving speeches in front of people.

"No, I'll give the speech," said Eleanor. "I was his best friend, after all. You can do the fencing performance."

"The what?"

"Fencing performance. For the beginning of the funeral. It will be like military honors. Like a twenty-one-gun salute but with a sword."

Owen was pretty sure his grandmother's funeral hadn't had a fencing performance. He would have heard about that. "I think a twenty-one-gun salute is for soldiers. Was your fish—was your fish in the army?"

"Of course not! He was in the *navy*. The fish navy. Very secret."

Owen wasn't sure how he was supposed to respond.

"And the fish navy does fencing at funerals," said Eleanor.

"The problem is," said Owen, "I can't fence by myself. I have to have a partner. That's how fencing works."

Eleanor wrinkled her nose in thought and bounced on her toes, which made all her pink glitter sparkle. "Okay. You teach me fencing this afternoon, and I'll help you perform the fencing part of the funeral. We can do it together."

"Okay," said Owen.

"Let me find a good sword," said Eleanor. She went inside.

Owen stood in the yard next to the bowl of dead goldfish. He had a lot of questions. A *lot*. What was the goldfish's name? Was there really such a thing as a fish navy? (He was pretty sure there was not.) What if he cried at the funeral? (He didn't think he would, but he'd heard that people did.) After the funeral, would the fish go to heaven? What was fish heaven like? Was it different than people heaven, where his grandmother was?

And most of all: What was life going to be like from now on, with this strange girl living in the apartment below him? She had just talked Owen into fencing at a fish funeral. What would she convince him of next?

Chapter 3
Eleanor

Eleanor ran inside to find her dad in the kitchen. He swiped crumbs from his mouth. "Hey, want a cookie, *corazoncito*?"

"Are those from Owen's mom?"

"Yes. Chocolate chip."

Chocolate chip was Eleanor's favorite.

Dad said, "So, are we having the funeral tonight?"

Eleanor said, "What is a funeral where you don't bury someone?"

"That's called a memorial service." Dad kept opening boxes, cookie in one hand. He did not seem to be listening all the way. "When do you want to do the funeral?"

"After supper. Owen's doing the fencing."

"The what?" Dad was listening a lot now.

"With a sword."

"For the funeral?"

"Yes. And I'm the minister. And you're in charge of playing guitar and singing something a fish would like. In Spanish, please. We need to say goodbye in both languages. It'll be very official."

"I can do that." Dad's mouth trembled. Suddenly Eleanor realized he must be trying not to cry. She was surprised. She didn't know he loved Scrumpy so much.

She patted his hand. "It's okay, Dad. God is in charge." It was what the minister had said at Great-Grandpa's funeral last year. That funeral didn't have any swords. Hers would be better. "God *is* in charge, right?" she said. "Even of a fish?"

"Even of a fish." He stood next to her at the counter, and they each ate another cookie, and then Dad covered the plate with plastic wrap. "We'd better save some for Mom." He looked at his watch. "Time for more unpacking." Aaron's and Alicia's voices drifted from the bedrooms.

Eleanor said, "Owen and I will be outside practicing for the memorial funeral show."

Dad's mouth jiggled again. "Okay, sweetie."

But before she could go out, she needed lightsabers. Owen brought the fishbowl inside just as Eleanor discovered—in a kitchen box—the perfect practice lightsabers: lasagna noodles. Uncooked, lasagna was stiff and flat, and if they taped a few pieces together, the swords were the right length.

In the backyard, though, the lasagna kept breaking every time they stabbed each other (which Owen called "lunging"). The lasagna sabers even broke when they *didn't* stab each other with them. They used more tape.

Finally Owen said, "This isn't working."

Owen was the sword expert, after all. "What should we do instead?" Eleanor asked.

"Well," said Owen, looking around, "sticks might work."

The yard was full of sticks. Big trees lined the back fence line—and there was the pine tree in the front. Sticks *every*where. And lots of weeds.

"Who does the yard work here?" Eleanor asked.

Owen shrugged. "I guess we do. The people who live here."

Eleanor frowned. Clearly Owen's family didn't have very high standards. "At my house," she said, "we pick up sticks so that my dad can mow. And we pull weeds," she added, looking at the dandelions.

"You mean your *old* house," said Owen.

"Where you used to live."

Eleanor glared. "And there's a tree house in the backyard. I'm going back there."

"To visit?"

"To live." Then she wished she hadn't said so much, because right away Owen wanted to know when her family was moving again.

What if he said something to her parents?

"It's a secret," she said quickly. "You have to promise not to tell, or I won't tell you any more. In fact, I'll make you forget everything I already told you."

"You can do that?"

"*Promise* not to tell."

"I promise." But he didn't look very happy about it.

"So the secret is," she said, swinging her new sword to test it, "I'm going to run away back to my old house. I'm going to bury

Scrumpy the Fourth there, and I'm going to live in the tree house."

"Your parents will let you?"

He sounded worried, like he might tell on her. She narrowed her eyes and looked sternly at him. "They will adjust to it," she said. "After I move back. People are flexible."

"You didn't tell them?"

"That's why it's a secret. And you can't tell either. You promised."

He nodded slowly. "I promised." Then he said, "What about the funeral?"

"What about it?"

"If you're burying Scrumpy at your old house, why are we doing a funeral here?"

"It's a *memorial* funeral. That's how they

work," said Eleanor. She wasn't quite sure that was right. To change the subject, she plunged her stick out in front of her and made a stance, using the words Owen had just taught her. "On guard! Are you ready?"

"Ready for what?"

"Let's fight!" she said. She swished her sword, making the buzzing noise that lightsabers make and standing in the fencing

stance she'd just learned. She shuffled forward and swung wildly. He brought his sword underneath and jabbed her lightly in the stomach. As she collapsed, clutching her heart, she said, "Owen! I . . . am . . . your . . . father!" Then she crumpled to the ground and lay still.

Her eyes were closed like Vader's when his mask came off, and she could hear the wind rustle in the trees and feel the long grass tickling her arms. Fencing was fun. It was too bad she'd have to stop practicing it with Owen when she moved back home.

But she'd already decided. And Jedis were not quitters.

Chapter 4
Owen

Owen stood over Eleanor, worried. "Are you okay?" He didn't think he'd lunged at her that hard—but he didn't usually fence without fencing gear. And she'd lunged toward him at the same time.

Eleanor's eyes popped open. "I'm fine. I was doing Vader. From the old, old *Star Wars*." She made the weird breathing sound.

"That's pretty good," said Owen. "But you know Vader's evil, right? Don't you want to be

one of the good guys
Like Luke? Or Leia?
You should be
Leia. Or someone
from the new *Star
Wars*."

She ignored the
new *Star Wars* suggestion. "My hair doesn't
make buns."

"Oh." Her hair was too curly to look like
Leia's. But then again, she didn't exactly look
like Vader either.

"I think maybe I'm going to be a memorial
funeral preacher when I grow up," said
Eleanor, standing and brushing the twigs off
her pink leggings. "*And* Darth Vader."

"You're going to be an evil preacher?"

She wrinkled her nose. "Don't be silly. I'll be Vader when he's good."

Owen decided not to point out that good Vader was around for only about a minute of the movie.

They kept practicing, but the sticks didn't make great swords—mainly because Eleanor jabbed hard, and even though she didn't hit Owen very often, when she did, it hurt. A lot. When they needed bandages, Owen had an idea.

"I have an old pool noodle. Let's cut it in half and put it on the ends of the swords."

Eleanor wrinkled her nose, like she was about to say no.

"It'll look like the lighted part of a lightsaber."

"That's a great idea!" Eleanor said.

When they went inside, they found Owen's mom in her medic pants and shirt, hugging Owen's dad. They were laughing and dancing slowly in a circle, and the radio was playing dance music—the kind that parents and other old people like.

Owen's dad said, "I got royalties today!"

And Owen's mom said, "We'll celebrate on Saturday! I'm off to work now." She kissed Owen's dad and left.

Eleanor said, "You're royalty?"

Owen's dad grinned. "It means I got paid for my writing."

Owen added, "He only gets royalties about once in a zillion years, so we always celebrate. Are we going to go to Pizza King? Can Eleanor come?"

Eleanor bounced, eyes bright.

"Sure, maybe this weekend. But I need to ask her parents first. And," he said to Eleanor, "your family is invited here for supper tonight. Pasta. Lots to go around."

"My dad would love that," said Eleanor. "He's supposed to make dinner, and we can't even find the toilet paper."

Owen told his dad why they were practicing fencing, and Dad said he wanted to go to the funeral too. "I've never been to a funeral with fencing."

"My dad's going to play guitar and sing," said Eleanor. "And I'm going to preach. Maybe you can read some of your writing? Do you have a poem about a dead fish?"

"He only writes books," said Owen.

"I'll write a poem this afternoon," said Owen's dad. "A haiku."

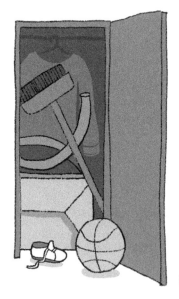

"Make sure it says that Scrumpy is in fish heaven. With his family."

"I'll do my best."

The kids went into the closet to find the pool noodle, and as they dug around,

Eleanor said, "Oh, I get it!"

"What?"

"Pizza *King*! It's for *royalty*!" said Eleanor.

Owen found the pool noodle. It was blue.

"Pizza King for royalty!" said Eleanor again. "Get it?"

"That's good," said Owen.

She knelt. "Make me royalty too."

Owen knew exactly what to do. He tapped her with the noodle, once on each shoulder. "I dub you . . . Queen Good Vader."

Eleanor said, "We fought with swords, and we're going to do a funeral together, and"—she lowered her voice to a loud whisper—"we have a secret plan together to help me get home. Because we are friends."

"Sure," said Owen. "Friends." But suddenly the closet felt too small, and his stomach hurt.

Chapter 5
Eleanor

Alicia had unpacked her room— which was also Eleanor's room. Eleanor got the closet, and the bed next to the big window. Alicia got the bed away from the window, but she also got the nook that stuck out of the room like a thumb and had its own window. Not fair. A closet was okay—because of Narnia—but a nook with its own window was way better. Alicia had put her desk and chair in the nook and had tacked posters on her wall.

Eleanor looked at her side of the room. Yuck. Her boxes were piled at the foot of the bed. She didn't even know where her sheets were.

Alicia said, "You should do your walls. But don't steal my tacks."

Eleanor glared and walked out. She wasn't going to live here anyway.

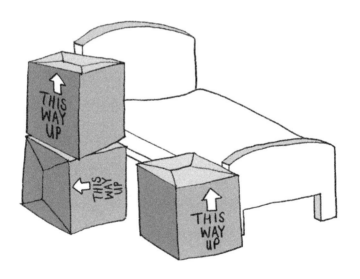

But what about Owen? said a little voice in her head. *Don't you want to live near him?* She tried not to listen to that little voice.

Aaron was unpacking too. He danced around with earbuds in his ears as he tossed clothes toward his dresser. It seemed like he didn't mind moving either. Suddenly Eleanor's stomach hurt.

Eleanor went to the kitchen. "I'm starving," she told her dad.

"When Mom's home, we'll eat. If I can find the pots . . . and the pasta . . . and the forks." He grinned at her expression. "I found the sauce!"

"Owen's dad said to come over for dinner. He's making pasta too. I guess he cooks like you." Eleanor's dad made pasta a *lot*. The pasta was always spaghetti with tomato sauce. His other meals were black beans and rice, and pancakes. His other meals after that were takeout.

"How fantastic," said Dad. "And that would definitely solve my current kitchen problems." He opened and peered into a box. "Oh! Here's the toilet paper!"

Eleanor took the toilet paper to the bathroom. When she returned, her dad said, "Now, *Cosita*, we need to decide about Scrumpy."

Poor Scrumpy still floated in his bowl on the counter, belly up. He was still dead. He did not smell great.

Dad said, "We could bury him. There's a spot in this backyard that would work nicely."

Eleanor shook her head. She wasn't going to bury Scrumpy away from the other Scrumpies.

Eleanor's dad opened a box and found spoons, forks, and knives. "We could flush him—"

"Uh-uh," said Eleanor. "No way."

Dad put the silverware away in a small drawer. He said, "You can have a day to decide. We can . . . keep him in the freezer until then." He didn't sound very excited. "But only a day or two. Your mom won't like this."

"Okay," Eleanor said. Mom could adjust. Scrumpy would only be in the freezer overnight. Tomorrow Eleanor would bring him home for the burial. And she'd move into her tree house.

Suddenly she thought of Owen again. It was like the little voice in her head was yelling at her: If she moved into the tree house, she and Owen couldn't play anymore. He couldn't teach her fencing. She couldn't teach him—well, all the things she knew. Like how to build things and how to raise goldfish. She'd miss Owen. He had made her a queen Jedi knight.

No. It didn't matter. She was leaving—for her real home. She frowned at her dad's unpacking. "The *old* silverware drawer had dividers."

Dad sighed. He did that a lot lately. "Maybe you should put your toys away."

Eleanor went back to her room. She didn't feel like unpacking. Her box of toys sat in the closet. Alicia said, "I moved it there. It was on my floor."

Eleanor sat in the closet and opened the box of toys. She didn't have dolls. She had building sets: Legos and blocks and Erector sets and even a little wooden trebuchet that she had built with her dad on her last birthday. A trebuchet was like a catapult, only better. And it was pronounced *tray-byou-shay*, which just wasn't right.

She dug down in the box for the pulleys and rope she'd used in her old room so that Aaron's Millennium Falcon could fly and escape from Darth Vader. Building that contraption had involved nails in the ceiling and a very long Time Out.

THUMP.

Something was hitting the ceiling.

"What's that?" said Alicia.

Eleanor thought she knew. She dragged Alicia's chair over to the closet.

"Hey," said Alicia. "What are you doing?"

"Shhhh!" Eleanor climbed on the chair. But she was still too short to reach the ceiling.

THUMP again! Eleanor listened. A small voice floated from the ceiling. It was saying . . .

it was saying . . . , *"OPEN YOUR WINDOW!"*

Eleanor ran to her window and yanked it open. There wasn't a screen, so she stuck her head out and looked straight up. There was Owen!

"Michael and I have the bedroom right above you!" he said.

"Michael?"

"My little brother. He was taking a nap. Now he's awake. See?" Owen disappeared and a smaller kid stuck his head out the window and waved. His hair was squished on one side from sleeping.

"I'm not little!" he yelled cheerfully. "I'm already five!"

Owen pulled Michael out of the window

and stuck his own head back out. He said, "We can send messages by thumping in the closet. I know about secret codes. I did a whole unit on them."

"You did?" Homeschooling suddenly sounded *way* interesting.

"Yes. We can decide what one thump means, or two quick thumps plus one slow thump, or anything like that, and we'll make a whole secret code."

From her side of the room, Alicia said, "That's a really annoying secret code for everyone else. *Thump thump thump* all the time. Also, you can't reach the ceiling."

Eleanor pulled her head back inside and studied her window. She stuck her head out and studied Owen's window. She had an idea. "I'm coming up."

Upstairs, Owen brought her to his and Michael's room. A bunk bed stood on one side of the room and bookshelves and toy shelves on the other side. Eleanor gasped. "You have tons of books!"

"Our dad is a writer," said Michael sadly. "We have to have a lot of books."

"Did you have an idea for messages?" said Owen.

Nodding, Eleanor studied the window in Owen's room. She said, "We can send messages by pulley!"

Chapter 6
Owen

Owen's dad said they could all play in Owen and Michael's room, and to please leave him alone for a while so he could write his chapter. Which was kind of perfect.

Owen helped Eleanor put together a pulley that would reach from his window to hers. He'd never built a pulley before.

"We just need to attach it, right?" said Owen, after Eleanor explained how it worked. "To the ceiling or something?"

"We'll get in trouble," said Michael. "Can I help?"

Eleanor handed Michael a plastic spaceship. "You can hold this for us. The notes go in here."

It was the Millennium Falcon, Han Solo's spaceship. Owen knew it right away. He had three books with the Millennium Falcon in them.

Eleanor explained how the pulley had been set up in her old room with nails in the ceiling.

"Well . . . ," said Owen. "We once put a nail in my wall to hang my corkboard. But the ceiling. . ."

"Big trouble," said Michael. He zoomed the spaceship around the room.

"Would it take more than one nail?" asked Owen. One might be okay.

"Probably ten nails," said Michael. "Or twenty-ten."

Eleanor said, "Less than ten. Maybe. Depends if chunks of ceiling fall down." She hitched her thumbs in her pockets and stared up.

Chunks of ceiling sounded bad. But should he stop Eleanor? *Could* he stop her? Should he . . . tell on her? Having friends was hard. "How about . . . maybe another option?" he said.

Eleanor kept studying the ceiling. She didn't answer.

Owen looked too. He studied the ceiling, then the window. "Oh! What about the curtain hooks?"

Eleanor grinned. She turned to Owen. "That's *genius*," she said.

Up near the ceiling were two big hooks, one on each side of the window, to hold up a curtain rod. But there was no rod and no curtain, only blinds. The two big hooks stuck out of the wall, doing nothing. Just asking to hold up a pulley.

Owen and Eleanor borrowed a kitchen chair. Then they ran downstairs and borrowed Aaron because they still couldn't reach the hooks. Aaron stood on the chair and looped the pulley over a curtain hook, winked at them, and went back downstairs.

Then Michael gave Eleanor the spaceship, and she tied it on the end of the rope and lowered it out the window, draping the rope over the ledge that stuck out just far enough to keep the ship from hitting the house. The Millennium Falcon dangled in front of her bedroom window. Eleanor raced down to her room. She reached out and poked the ship, making it sway. "Pull the rope," said Eleanor, "and make it soar back up!"

"Okay!" said Owen. He pulled, and the spaceship rose just like it was flying. Then he had an idea. "Don't leave yet! Wait there!"

He ran to his desk, pulled out a piece of paper, and scribbled Olleh! woh era uoy?

Then he folded it up very small, opened the door to the spaceship, and put the note inside.

Owen pulled, and the Millennium Falcon descended to Eleanor.

A few minutes later, Eleanor was back in his room. "That note was in code, right? I figured it out! Every word was backward!"

Olleh!
Woh era uoy?

"That was an easy code," said Owen. "But if we want it to be tricky, we should invent a code together. That way it will be something only we know."

"Yeah," said Eleanor. "Alicia figured your message out really quick too. We need a harder code so it's secret from spies."

Owen found his book on codes, and they looked through it. Finally they decided that they would pick a complicated code later. For today they would just have some secret phrases, like the way *The eagle has landed* means you've finished doing something important. That was one the code book had told them.

"How about *The goldfish has landed*?" Owen asked. "It could mean . . . I don't know . . ." He wasn't sure what they needed to say that was secret from everyone else.

"I'll need to let you know when we're doing

57

The Plan," said Eleanor.

"The Plan?" said Owen.

Eleanor glanced around, but no one was there except Michael, who had crawled under his bed, muttering about beavers and wolves and endless winter. All you could see were his feet. "The *Plan*," Eleanor whispered loudly. "The plan to run away back home. To bury Scrumpy and move back to the tree house."

"Are you sure . . . ?" Owen asked.

"Yes," said Eleanor. "And you promised not to tell. And to help me." She looked very stern.

Owen nodded slowly. He *had* promised not to tell. He didn't remember promising to help—but friends helped each other. What kind of friend would he be if he didn't help? Still, he wondered what his parents would think of his keeping this secret and helping with this plan.

"Excellent! All systems are go." Eleanor bounced on her toes. "How about *The goldfish is hungry* is the code for when I'm going to run away and ride the city bus to my old house? It's on the corner of Central Avenue and 31st Street. Can you figure out which bus I need?" She was talking very fast. "You're my trusty navigator—you're like Chewbacca, and I'm Han Solo. I'll send you a note tomorrow when it's time to go."

Everything was happening so fast. And Owen wasn't sure he liked being Chewbacca.

"Tomorrow?" He was hoping they could wait until—well, until forever.

"Yes, tomorrow. We'll go to play in the backyard, and then I'll escape."

Owen sighed and nodded. "The goldfish is hungry." He had promised, after all. But he really wished he hadn't.

Chapter 7
Eleanor

When Eleanor's mom came home from the store for the third time, everyone went upstairs to Owen's apartment for supper with Owen and Michael and Owen's dad. Owen's mom was still working—she was a paramedic, so she worked a lot of strange hours. Once every three days, she was gone all day and night.

The two families stood around the table. There were only really four places at the table, but Owen's dad had squished an extra chair in so all the bigger people, even Alicia, could sit down. "I thought Owen and Eleanor and Michael might like a picnic on the floor." In the living room, on a blanket, were three more plates and silverware and water cups.

"That will be great!" said Eleanor. Usually she was not allowed to eat on the floor because of spilling. She started toward the living room. Owen followed.

"Wait," said Owen's dad. He turned to Eleanor's parents. "We usually pray before we eat. Is that okay with you?"

"Of course," said Eleanor's mom. "We usually pray before meals too."

They all held hands (Eleanor had to hold Alicia's and her mom's), and Owen's dad said a prayer that was made up out of his own head. He called God *Spirit of Life*. He said God was like a mother and a father. And he asked God to bless the new friends in the apartment below. *That's us*, thought Eleanor. *Except I'm not staying.*

When they finished, she said, "That was a weird prayer."

Her dad said, "Eleanor."

"It wasn't how we pray," she explained to Owen and his family. "We say *God-is-great-and-God-is-good-and-we-thank-him-for-this-food-Amen*."

Eleanor's mother cleared her throat. "There are many ways to talk to God."

"Maybe God likes hearing different prayers," said Owen's dad. "All the same would get boring."

Eleanor nodded. That made sense.

"This pasta looks delicious!" said Dad.

It wasn't pasta like Eleanor's dad made. First of all, it wasn't spaghetti. It was short noodles that looked like little fat straws. Also, it wasn't covered in tomato sauce but instead was mixed with mushrooms and weird green

stuff and little globs of white
cheese. But the good
part was that there
was also macaroni and
cheese made from a box,

for people who didn't want the gross white globby cheese and the giant slimy-looking mushrooms. Eleanor ate mac and cheese, and so did Michael.

Also, there was warm bread and a big bowl of grapes, and there was a green leafy salad. Eleanor did not eat the salad.

Owen ate the grown-up pasta *and* the salad. He did not even pick out the vegetables. Eleanor didn't understand it. But he convinced her to try a mushroom by telling her that she was a spy in Jabba the Hutt's domain, and if she didn't eat the slug food, people would find out and she'd be caught. So she ate the slug food.

One bite.

And really? It wasn't too bad.

And Owen wasn't too bad either. In fact, he was awesome.

It was too bad that she couldn't live downstairs from Owen *and* live at her old house.

But she had to pick one, and she had already picked her old house. Jedi queens did not go back on their decisions.

Eleanor swallowed the slug food and stuck out her tongue. "Yuck. Mushrooms are gross."

Chapter 8
Owen

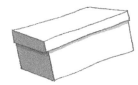 After dinner, everyone went to the backyard for the fish funeral. They brought folding chairs and put them in two nice rows so that Owen's dad and Michael and Eleanor's parents and her big sister and big brother could sit. "How long will this take?" asked Alicia. "I'm supposed to call Millie tonight. My best friend," she added to Owen.

Eleanor said, "You call her every night."

Alicia ignored Eleanor. She turned to Owen's dad to explain. "She's coming over on her bike tonight to say hi."

Eleanor said, "But tonight is the funeral, and it will take a *long time*."

"Girls," said their mom in a warning voice— just like the warning voice Owen's mom used on him and Michael. "Shall we begin? Where's the fish?"

Eleanor jumped up. "In the freezer. I'll get him."

As she left, Eleanor's mom said, "Rafael. . . ." She spoke in the same kind of voice Owen's mom used when his dad one time used up all their butter to make muffins. And Eleanor's dad said, "I triple-bagged him. What else could I do?" And then Eleanor's mom shook her head and smiled, just like Owen's mom did when she took a bite of a buttery muffin.

Eleanor came back with the fish in a shoe box (and in its baggies). The shoebox said COFFEN on the side. She said, "Dad, you should start with singing, like in church. And then poetry. And then Owen and I will fence."

"Like in church," murmured Alicia. Eleanor's mom gave Alicia a Look.

"Sounds good," said Eleanor's dad. He sang something in Spanish. And even though Owen was learning Spanish and already knew *¿Cómo estás?* And *Me llamo Owen*, he didn't understand the words. But the music was nice, and all of Eleanor's family joined in on the chorus. Owen nudged Eleanor and gave her a questioning look. She translated, "The chickens say *pío pío pío*." He nodded, even though he didn't know what that meant. Chickens said *cluck cluck cluck*—didn't they?

Also, it wasn't a song about a fish. But everyone seemed to like it, and by the end, Owen could sing *pío pío pío* too.

Then Owen's dad read a very short and sad poem. It compared Scrumpy to a butterfly.

Then it was time to fence. Owen was a little nervous because he didn't think he liked doing shows. Also, when Eleanor got excited, she didn't always remember the routine. But they made it through with only one mistake, where she twirled instead of blocking and Owen accidentally stabbed her. She fell to the ground and pretended to die, and she was really good at dying, so it was all okay. She even said, "Scrumpy . . . I . . . am . . . your . . . father" at the very end, before she rolled her eyes back in her head and clunked her sword to the ground.

Everyone clapped. Owen was glad it was done.

Eleanor gave a speech. It was hard to follow, but mostly she said there were four Scrumpies, and she didn't know if there would ever be another one like the ones who had already lived. And she said this was a memorial funeral with no burying and not a *funeral* funeral with burying. And all the Scrumpies needed to be buried together so that they could go to heaven together. When she said that, her parents did not look super happy. And then she said that Scrumpy died of sadness because he had to move. That also did not make her parents look happy. And she said that Scrumpy was a good fish—a *golden* fish—who God loved.

"The End," said Eleanor. "The funeral is over. You can go now."

Alicia jumped up.

"Maybe we could sing again?" said Eleanor's dad. "One last song."

Alicia sat back down. Slowly.

Eleanor's dad said, "In memory of Scrumpy." He strummed again, and it was a tune that Owen knew, and this time they all sang in English, as much of the words as they could remember: *"All things bright and beautiful, all creatures great and small, all things wise and wonderful, the Lord God loves them all."*

Then the funeral was really over. Owen realized that from now on, if anyone ever asked him if he'd gone to a funeral, he could say he'd been to two of them. And he could say that he remembered one of them very well. And it was a good one.

As they put the chairs away, Eleanor whispered in his ear, "The Plan. Tomorrow."

Suddenly Owen was sorry the memorial funeral was over so soon.

Chapter 9
Eleanor

After the funeral it was time for bed. Eleanor lay in her old bed in the strange new room. Alicia had to read in the living room so Eleanor could sleep, and Alicia was grumpy about it. Eleanor thought about how happy her sister would be when she had a room all to herself again.

Eleanor's mom read to her from the second Narnia book, which is about two kids who run away from home and live on a ship and sail around the world. Eleanor lay back on her pillow and listened.

Eleanor's mom closed the book at the end of the chapter. "You know, what you said in your funeral talk . . . ?"

"My sermon?" Eleanor waited for a compliment. It was a great sermon. She would definitely become a preacher when she grew up. A preacher part time and Darth Vader full time. Or the other way around. *Good* Vader, she reminded herself, thinking of what Owen had said.

"What you said in your sermon," her mother said, "wasn't quite right. Not all the way. Scrumpy doesn't need to be with his family in order to go to heaven. In fact, lots of people are buried far away from their families."

"Like soldiers?"

"Sure. And other people too. Immigrants. Refugees. Or just people who've moved far away from where they were born. God knows where they are, even if they're a long way away from home."

Eleanor nodded. That meant God knew where she was too. She thought of God maybe having a phone with a Google map and she was a blue dot moving from the old house to the duplex. God knew where she was, even at the new house. She was always the blue dot, and God could always find her.

But that didn't mean she should *stay* at the

new house.

Her mom brushed back her curls and kissed her forehead. "Good night, sweetie."

"Good night, Mom." Eleanor fell asleep imagining herself as a blue dot looking for a path back to her old home.

The next day Eleanor's mom stayed home from work again, so they unpacked and put things away all day long. There was no way to run off and start a new life. Eleanor sent a note up to Owen on the pulley: NO HUNGRY FISH TODAY.

All the unpacking made Eleanor think of something she hadn't thought of before. It was this: She couldn't take all her clothes and toys to the tree house. She would have to leave a lot of things behind. She made a list of all the things she *wouldn't* need:

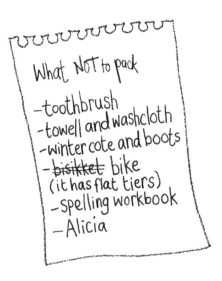

What NOT to pack

-toothbrush
-towell and washcloth
-winter cote and boots
- ~~bisikket~~ bike
(it has flat tiers)
-spelling workbook
-Alicia

Studying the list, she saw a problem. She didn't want to leave very many things behind. And even more important, she didn't want to leave any *people* behind. She didn't want to move away from her family—not even Alicia.

She crumpled up the paper. So *what* if she couldn't decide what stuff to leave behind right now? There were still a lot of plans to make. She could decide what to take and what to leave behind later. Maybe—oh! maybe she could come back to visit after she moved to the tree house? Sure, she could do that. And she could change her clothes here when the clothes she was wearing got dirty. Maybe every two weeks or so. And she could pick up a toy or book if she needed it. So really, she didn't need to pack hardly anything.

She hummed. Problem solved.

That night just before supper, Owen thumped on the ceiling three times, and she ran upstairs. "I made an improvement to the pulley!" he said.

Michael was bouncing on his bottom bunk. "I thought of it," he said. "Owen, tell her I thought of it."

Owen said, "Michael thought of it. But I *made* it."

Eleanor looked at the pulley. The spaceship was still there. Now, under the spaceship hung a string, and clipped to the string was a little basket with a lid. "In case we want to send anything bigger than a note," said Owen.

Eleanor frowned. "The Millennium Falcon can't jump into hyperspace with a basket."

"True," said Owen. "So when they jump, we'll need to take the basket off. It'll be part of the orders to the crew. *Eject storage unit. Execute jump!*"

Eleanor considered. That sounded like something Han Solo might really say. *Eject storage unit. Execute jump!* "Okay," she said. But then she thought, *okay* wasn't enough. A basket was a big deal. They could send *anything* back and forth now—anything small enough to fit in a basket, anyway. She could think of so many things—books and toys and art projects and so many other little things that she could send Owen and he could send her. At least until she moved back to her real home. "This is *great*!" she said.

Owen grinned.

That night after supper, Owen sent down five brownies that his dad had made. They were wrapped in a cloth napkin and were still warm. There was a note that said, Enjoy, everyone! so Eleanor had to share them.

Eleanor sent the napkin back. She also sent a friendship bracelet for Owen. She had braided it months ago, but she didn't have anyone to give it to then. And now she did. She wrote, "Enjoy, Owen!" on the note she taped to the bracelet. And she also wrote Friendship brasslet with an arrow, in case he didn't know what it was.

Then Owen sent a note that said Thank you and good night, and Eleanor sent a note that said Thank you too and good night too because she had forgotten to say thank you for the brownies before.

Eleanor went to bed, thinking how much fun it was to live underneath someone who had a pulley attached to their curtain rod.

And feeling a little sad that she would be moving away.

Chapter 10
Owen

Owen, meanwhile, had a good day. Eleanor had sent a note postponing the plan (NO HUNGRY FISH TODAY), and he and Dad and Michael went swimming, even though Lake Harriet was still cold. And then he and Michael improved the pulley (he did the work, even though Michael had the idea), and they saw Eleanor again. And there were brownies.

But Eleanor was still planning to leave.

The next morning when Owen woke up, he heard Michael eating breakfast with Dad. He stretched his toes and arms as far as they would go and listened to all the morning sounds. The side window—the one with the screen—let him hear the birds singing and the squirrels chattering. The leaves rustled. In the kitchen, Michael was telling Dad about a big ferocious monster at the zoo, and Dad was saying it sounded like maybe a sea otter and they could look it up after breakfast.

Owen got up. Dad said, "Good morning. *Quiet* morning." Which meant that Mom had just gotten home from work and needed to sleep. Dad said, "We'll have reading time right after breakfast."

Dad poured Owen's cereal, and Owen said a silent prayer. *(Thank you for Eleanor because she is fun! And please make Michael stop kicking me.)* As he was eating, Owen said, "Can I play with Eleanor today?"

"Me too!" said Michael.

"She's *my* friend, not yours," said Owen.

Owen's dad took a sip of coffee and ran his fingers through his hair. He looked tired. "Friends," he said, "are for sharing. I believe you can all play together." Then before Owen could argue, he added, "She seems nice."

"She is," said Owen. "And she knows how to make pulleys, but she doesn't know how to fence, so we're going to teach each other lots of stuff."

"I bet she doesn't know how to spit with aiming," said Michael. "I bet I could teach her."

"Nope," said Dad. "Nope nope nope. Think of something else."

Michael thought, mouth full of cereal.

"Owen," Dad said, "do you and Eleanor have any plans for that pulley? Something top secret?" He grinned.

"Um . . . just notes," said Owen. "Maybe in code, if we figure out a code we like." He wanted to say, *"The goldfish is hungry* means she's planning to run away." But he didn't say it. He looked down at his cereal bowl. The little O's stared back at him. He knew he should tell Dad about Eleanor's Plan. But he had promised Eleanor not to tell. And now she wanted him to *help* her run away. The little O's glared at him.

He dunked them with his spoon.

"Dad," he said, "Eleanor used to live on the corner of Central Avenue and 31st Street. She told me. Where is that?"

"Let's see," said Dad. He brought his phone to the table and typed into the map app. "Right here." The blue dot flashed on the spot.

Owen pushed the directions button, like he did whenever they went places.

"How would you get there?" asked Dad. "See if you can figure it out."

This was too easy. Owen clicked on the bus icon and read the directions. "The 67 bus south. Then the 34 east. Then walk two blocks south."

Dad checked. "Good job." He pocketed the phone. "Now, finish your breakfast."

"Pillbugs!" said Michael. "I could teach Eleanor. I bet she doesn't know where to find the best pillbugs."

"I bet she doesn't *want* to know," said Owen.

———————————

Reading time was nice. Dad read four stories that Michael picked—books with pictures on every page—and then he read a chapter from Narnia. That book actually had a longer name, but Owen and Michael both called it the

Narnia book. A couple of weeks earlier, Owen had noticed a collection of small paperbacks on the shelf. The covers had monsters and swords and lions and things like that, but when he opened the books, they had lots of words and looked very grown up, with hardly any pictures. He took the first book off the shelf and asked his dad to read it to him. And to his surprise, Dad said yes.

While Dad read Narnia, Owen and Michael lay on their bellies on the floor and colored. Owen colored a picture of Aslan the lion *right as they were reading about him*. It was the best thing ever.

But when he went back into his and Michael's room, the spaceship dangled outside the window.

Inside the Falcon was a note. It said,

THE GOLDFISH IS HUNGRY!!!!

(After lunch)

(from Eleanor)

Chapter 11
Eleanor

Eleanor had been up for hours. *Hours.* Her mom had sent her back to bed twice because it was too early to get up, and then after her mom left for work, her dad sent her back to bed one more time. Finally she was allowed to get up because Alicia was mad at all the noise Eleanor was making getting in and out of bed. But she had to sit quietly in the living room and read a book without talking until at least seven a.m.

Seven a.m. is a long time away when it is only 6:27 and you have already been up forever, waiting for morning to come.

Eleanor tried to read, but she needed to *do* things. She got out her markers and drew a big drawing of her tree house, the one behind her old home, with lots of details, like the rope ladder and the two windows and the red roof.

She even added some details that weren't in the real tree house, like a pulley for carrying snacks up and down, and flowerpots in the window, and a red chimney in the roof with little friendly curls of smoke coming out. Last of all, she wrote MY HOME! under the tree house, in bright pink letters, because pink was her favorite. Then it was seven a.m.

Dad got up and made some breakfast for Alicia and Eleanor. (Aaron was still sleeping. In his own room. By himself.)

After breakfast, Dad had work to do in his office (in a corner of Mom and Dad's bedroom), because even though he didn't teach in the summer, he still had reading and writing to do. Being a college professor used up a lot of thinking time. He asked Eleanor to give him one hour to work, and then they could explore the new neighborhood.

Eleanor shook her head. "I don't want to explore the new neighborhood."

"Hmm," said Dad. "Well, maybe after lunch then."

"Can I play with Owen?"

"It's too early. Maybe after lunch."

Uuuuuuuugh. After lunch was forever. And she'd already had quiet time since super early in the morning. How much quiet time could one kid handle?

Eleanor went to her room—her *and Alicia's* room, that is—and she sat on her bed and thought. Then she wrote a note. A very important note. She put it in the Millennium Falcon and sent it up to Owen. It said, THE GOLDFISH IS HUNGRY!!!! (After lunch).

As an afterthought, she added (from Eleanor) just to make sure he knew who the note was from.

She waited.

Nothing happened. Maybe he was still sleeping. She waited some more. Nothing happened again.

She decided to get a message to him another way. Maybe she could throw something at his window. Something soft-ish. Hard enough to make a noise but soft enough not to break glass.

But when she threw her pillow at Owen's window, it didn't go up enough, and she barely caught the pillow before it fell all the way to the ground.

She decided to build a machine that would throw things up to Owen. For the rest of the morning, she took apart her trebuchet and built a bigger, stronger one. She was pretty sure that if she could launch things straight up, Owen could learn to catch them, and with practice they would both become all-star baseball players.

When she got the trebuchet rebuilt, she tested it by launching her pink rectangle-shaped eraser.

But she couldn't get the trebuchet to throw the eraser straight up—she could only get it to throw *farther*. And *harder*.

The second time she hit Alicia, who was sitting on her bed reading, Alicia told her to get out.

"No. It's my room too!"

"Then stop throwing stuff at me!"

"I'm an engineer. I have to test things. Don't tell me what to do anyway."

"Daaaaaaad!"

And the morning was done.

Alicia and Eleanor both got to help with lunch. Eleanor got to peel the eggs and mash them into egg salad, which was fun. Alicia got to set the table and pour milk, which was less fun. Aaron got to wake up and take a shower.

Just as they were about to eat, Owen knocked at the door. Dad said Eleanor could play after lunch.

"Michael and my dad are in the yard," said Owen, "looking for pillbugs, and then my mom will wake up and then I have to eat lunch too."

Eleanor said, "Are you going to eat pillbugs?"

"No!" said Owen. "Michael thought you might like to see them. After lunch," he added to Eleanor's dad.

Eleanor's dad said, "Pillbugs after lunch." Eleanor could tell he didn't know exactly what *pillbugs* meant. Even though he had lived in the United States a long time, sometimes he still didn't recognize a word. He pulled out his phone to check his English–Spanish dictionary. "Ah. Pillbugs. Yes. Perfect."

"Um," said Owen. "I just have something to ask Eleanor."

"One minute," said Dad.

"One minute," said Eleanor. She stepped out into the entryway with Owen and closed the door. "Did you get my message? *The goldfish is hungry*?" Suddenly everything seemed very exciting.

Owen didn't look excited. "Yes," he said. "Are you sure? I mean, you could just stay here."

"And bury Scrumpy away from his family? And away from his real house? And *my* real house?" Then, worried she'd hurt Owen's feelings, she said, "This is a nice duplex. But I want to go *home*."

Slowly Owen nodded. "Okay then."

"I have money for the bus," said Eleanor. "But I don't know which bus to take."

Owen said slowly, "I figured out the buses this morning."

"You did?" Eleanor had taken the bus only a few times in her whole life. What if she took the wrong bus by accident? What if she got off at the wrong bus stop? Then she had an idea. "Hey, you can come with me. To help bury Scrumpy. And I can show you my house." She tried to make it sound like an adventure.

Owen stood still for a minute, thinking and frowning like he was making a big decision. Then he nodded. "I'll go with you." But he didn't sound happy.

No matter. He'd love the tree house when he saw it. "Okay! Let's go right after lunch!"

Owen nodded gloomily and went upstairs. Eleanor went inside to eat.

After lunch, Aaron biked to his job. Alicia biked to her friend Millie's house. Dad phoned Mom just to say hi.

Eleanor sat on her bed in her and Alicia's room—really just Alicia's room after today—and packed her backpack. Two granola bars she hadn't eaten at snack time yesterday and the day before. A full water bottle. A book, in case she wanted some quiet time in the tree house. Her money for bus fare. And on top,

the dead fish, frozen into a little fish rock and still triple-bagged. She'd gotten him out of the freezer when Dad was busy phoning Mom.

She looked around the room. Alicia had put posters on Eleanor's side of the room—of cats and dogs, because Alicia knew she loved animals. That was nice of her. She'd also put yellow tape on the floor to mark her side of the room so that Eleanor didn't step there. That was less nice.

But the spaceship window was on Eleanor's side of the room. Outside the window hung the rope of the Millennial Falcon, waiting to send another secret message. Beyond the rope she could see the backyard with its row of trees, weedy and shady almost like a real woods. On the ground were a lot of sticks for making lightsabers and rocks for building fairy gardens. Really, it was a good yard.

Dad poked his head into the room. "You going to Owen's to play?"

Not play. Run away. This afternoon. But somehow, now, the idea didn't make her happy.

She picked up her backpack. "I'm going."

Chapter 12
Owen

 Owen met Eleanor at the door, wishing he knew what to do to stop her from leaving.

She called out, "We're going to play in the backyard!"

Owen's mom appeared. She was dressed in normal clothes and had wet hair like she had just taken a shower. "If that's okay with your dad," she said to Eleanor.

"Me too!" said Michael.

Yes. Owen grinned. If Michael was outside

with them, then they wouldn't be able to run away.

But Owen's mom said, "Not you, Mister Mike. You have a haircut today." She herded him down the front stairs.

When they reached the shady part of the backyard, Eleanor tossed her backpack down. "See?" she said. "Everything's perfect. We're *meant* to escape."

It didn't feel like *escape* to Owen. It felt like *mistake*.

"Let's go now!" she said.

"We have to wait until Mom and Michael get down the street so they don't see us," said Owen.

"Okay. Hey, let's fence! You know, for old

times' sake." She leaped into position. Owen told her that the first person says *pray*, then the other person says *we*, and then the first person says *uh-lay*, and then you fight.

"Why do you say *pray* and *we* and all that?" asked Eleanor.

"It's French," said Owen. "So it doesn't really make sense. Maybe your dad would know?"

"He only knows Spanish," said Eleanor. "Like me. Only better," she admitted, "since he spoke Spanish when he was growing up."

"That's cool," said Owen.

"He grew up in Costa Rica. And they talk in Spanish."

"Does he miss Costa Rica? Do you ever visit? Do your grandma and grandpa still live there?" Owen had a lot of questions.

Eleanor laughed. "Yes, we visit, but not very often because plane tickets cost so much. One time our grandparents, Abuela and Abuelo, came here to visit us. Well, not *here*. To the old house." She threw down her sword, frowning. "I bet your mom and Michael are gone."

Owen thought about how much Eleanor missed the old house. He sighed. "Yeah. Okay. Let's go."

They only had to wait a couple of minutes for the bus. It was the 67, and it would take them to the 34. Owen showed Eleanor how to get a transfer ticket.

On the first bus, the bus driver knew Owen. He said, "You're a big man, riding the bus by yourself. Where are you going?" He grinned.

"To Eleanor's house," Owen said. Eleanor elbowed him, and he thought maybe he shouldn't have said anything. But he'd been surprised by the bus driver asking him questions.

On the next bus, no one asked them questions, except for one old lady who asked them what grade they were in and said her grandson was eight.

When they got off the 34, Owen was worried they might get lost, but Eleanor recognized the corner right away.

"This way!" she said. She hoisted her backpack over both shoulders and ran. Owen followed.

"See?" she yelled back at him. "That's my house! Isn't it the prettiest blue house you ever saw? And doesn't it have the prettiest yard?"

Then she skittered to a stop.

Only the front of the house was blue. The sides were white. And there were two guys on ladders with trays of white paint.

"What are they doing?" Eleanor's voice went up really high. "They're ruining the house! Stop!" she yelled, waving her arms and running toward the men on ladders.

"What's up?" said the closest one. He was young. The other man was old.

"Stop!" Eleanor screamed. "This house is supposed to be *blue*!"

The younger guy shrugged, and the older man said, "The new owners want it white. Got a work order right here." He patted his chest pocket. "White with red trim. It'll look real nice when it's done."

Eleanor was standing very still now, and her voice was cold and quiet. "What *else* did you change?"

The younger man shrugged and said, "Well, we tore down the old tree house before we started painting. And tomorrow—"

The man didn't get to finish his sentence. "*NOOOO!*" Eleanor sprinted to the backyard. Owen followed.

There was the tree, as tall and beautiful as Eleanor had described it.

Under the tree was a pile of ripped-up wood.

And *in* the tree: nothing. No tree house.

Eleanor cried. She sat right down in the backyard that wasn't hers anymore, and she cried. Owen sat down next to her and helped her shrug off her backpack and pulled out her water bottle. He didn't

know what else to do. The torn-down tree house was really sad. And Eleanor's plan to live there was dead.

They sat for a long time while Eleanor cried. Then they both drank out of the water bottle.

As they finished the water, Eleanor's dad

ran into the backyard and picked her up. He was crying too. Not real tears like Eleanor. But his eyes were red. Owen could tell.

Owen said, "I'm sorry." He meant about running away. And making Eleanor's dad worry. And probably his own parents too.

Eleanor's dad put his hand on Owen's shoulder like he understood. Then he put Eleanor down and phoned Owen's parents to say everything was okay.

Then he drove them home.

At home they found out that Owen's mom could yell and cry and hug at the same time. And that Michael was better at listening than they had thought. And that after Michael had told about The Plan to run away, Owen's mom had run to the bus stop, and Eleanor's dad had driven to the old house. And that in all, the running away lasted one hour and twenty-eight minutes.

And that they were in trouble for all of those minutes.

Finally Owen's mom said, "What were you thinking, young man?"

"I'm sorry," Owen said. "I just wanted to be a good friend. A good friend helps. I didn't want her to be mad at me."

Owen's mom nodded. "That's a hard one." She sat on the sofa in the living room and pulled Owen onto her lap. They just sat for a long time, and then Owen's mom said, "I think a good friend will be your friend even if you don't help her do dangerous things. And I think Eleanor's a good friend."

Owen thought about that. Eleanor *was* a good friend. And he'd be a good friend too, from now on.

Chapter 13
Eleanor and Owen

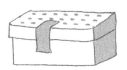 In the downstairs kitchen, Eleanor fished Scrumpy out of the backpack and put him on the counter. He was still in the three baggies. He was mostly thawed. He did not look too good.

In fact, Scrumpy looked really, really bad.

Eleanor's dad covered his mouth and swallowed. Then he moved the cookie plate to the table, away from the fish. "Eleanor. *Querida*. Please explain."

"We were going to bury him—with all the other Scrumpies. And then I was going to live in the tree house. At my *real* home." Her lip quivered.

Dad sat at the table and motioned Eleanor to sit next to him. "Sweetheart, do you know where *my* home is?"

"The old house?"

"No."

"Here?" She wrinkled her nose. "It's yellow."

"Not here."

Eleanor said, "Then where?" Suddenly she thought of something. "Is your real home in Costa Rica? Do you want to go back to where you were born?" And what if he did? What then? What if her own dad wanted to run away just like she did? That would be terrible.

"No worries," said Dad. He brushed her cheek. "My real home isn't in Costa Rica. My home is here with my family. Wherever my family is, that's my home."

Eleanor sighed with relief. She took a cookie—a big, round, perfect one with lots of chocolate chips.

Dad said, "But that's not even the whole truth. Here on earth, we never have a permanent home. Your mom left Grandma and Grandpa Lohman to work in Costa Rica. I left my house with Abuela and Abuelo when I went to college, and I moved away even further when I married your mom and we came here.

Someday you'll leave your family too: to go to college, take a job, get married—something. Your home on earth might change a dozen times."

"Or a hundred," said Eleanor, breaking the cookie into little pieces.

"Let's hope not," said her dad. "But you're right. You could have a lot of homes on earth. But your real home is always with God. God always loves you." He hugged her. "And so do I."

"And Mom loves me?"

"And Mom loves you. And Aaron loves you. And even Alicia loves you."

"But—" she said. "What about Scrumpy? What are we going to do about him?"

Dad stole one of her broken pieces and popped it in his mouth. "I have an idea about that."

They buried Scrumpy in the backyard of the duplex, and Eleanor and Owen painted a special brick to be the gravestone. The brick had a drawing of two lightsabers on it, crossed. And it also had waves and fish food and sailboats painted all around the sides, because those were things Scrumpy liked. And if Eleanor ever moved again, she could take the brick to the new house. If she wanted to.

Eleanor and Owen were grounded from walking around the neighborhood by themselves. For the rest of the week, they stayed in the backyard or inside. Owen and Michael finished the first Narnia book, but Eleanor hadn't finished the second one yet. She started hers over so that they could all listen to it together. Saturday they had supper at Pizza King. And they played together every day.

A week after the running away, Eleanor's dad invited Owen to go on an errand, which was weird. And Eleanor wasn't invited, which was even weirder. And they did not come back until suppertime. Aaron and Alicia made grilled cheese sandwiches and tomato soup from a can, and Eleanor's mom came home from work, and they all started eating.

Then, *finally*, Eleanor's dad and Owen walked in the door. Owen's mom and dad and Michael joined them.

Owen carried a cardboard box.

Owen held the box very carefully in both hands, and his face was bright, like he was about to explode. The box was a big shoebox, the size for winter boots, and it was taped shut with one piece of silver tape, and it had little round holes in the top just big enough to stick your pinky finger through.

Eleanor's dad said, "It's a surprise for the whole family—but mostly for Eleanor, because she misses Scrumpy."

"And I picked her out," said Owen.

Her?

"Ohhhhhh! It's a new fish!" shouted Michael.

"Not in a cardboard box with holes," said Alicia.

"Is that . . . ?" said Eleanor. She stood still in the middle of the room. She didn't dare hope too hard. "Is that . . . ?"

"Open it," said her dad.

"Open it!" yelled Michael.

Owen held out the box. But by then Eleanor already knew. Because the box was *meowing*.

She opened it. Inside was a kitten, tiny and fuzzy and stripy.

Owen said, "She's orange, just like Scrumpy. I picked her for you. She was the only orange one."

Eleanor was too excited to say anything. Her eyes shone.

Eleanor and Owen sat cross-legged on the floor next to each other, and Eleanor's dad reached into the box and put the kitten on her lap. It meowed. It crawled from her lap to Owen's and back again. It licked both their hands. It was so fuzzy and little.

And everyone was laughing and talking, and there was a litter box and a food bowl and a water bowl and cat toys that looked like little mice. And the kitten had the softest little pink pads on her feet and tiny little claws that prickled when she walked on your bare legs. And she had whiskers that tickled when you put your face next to hers.

After a while, all the grown-ups went to the backyard with lemonade and with Michael. Alicia went to her friend Millie's, and Aaron went back to his room. Owen and Eleanor and the kitten were alone in the living room.

"She's the best kitten ever," said Owen.

"She is," Eleanor said. "We're going to share her."

"Really?" said Owen.

"Yes," said Eleanor. "Because we live in the same house, and you're my best friend. Right?"

He nodded.

"We'll feed her and take care of her together. We'll train her to be a Jedi cat. She'll live at both apartments."

"My mom is allergic to cats," said Owen. "We can't have a kitten."

"Oh," said Eleanor, who had been imagining how to fit the kitten into the pulley basket or on the trebuchet to launch her from bedroom to bedroom. "Well, okay then. She'll live here, and you'll just have to visit all the time."

Owen grinned. That would work fine. It would be like having a cat but without his mom sneezing.

"She needs a name," said Eleanor. "I know exactly the right one."

Owen said, "Scrumpy the Fifth?"

Eleanor shook her head, smiling. "Guess again."

Owen thought about all the fun things they'd done since they met—reading Narnia, building Lego robots and play dough monsters, rebuilding the trebuchet to make it throw heavy things like tomatoes. He thought about fencing. He thought about *Star Wars* and all the times he defeated Darth Vader or (if Vader was good that day) fought *with* Vader to defeat the Dark Side. "Um . . . Good Vader?" he said. "Jedi Queen?"

She shook her head, grinning. "One more guess."

Owen thought all the way back to the day they met, when Eleanor was standing on the sidewalk holding her fish up to the sunlight and promising to bring him home.

He thought about the pulley they rigged later that day out his bedroom window. He thought about riding the bus together and the empty tree and Eleanor crying. He thought about secret codes. And he thought about all the things that a cat might secretly *mean*: home and family and love and belonging. And then he knew.

"Oh!" said Owen. "The kitten's name is *Goldfish*!"

It was the perfect name.

Later, Owen was almost ready to go to bed when he got a message from the Millennium Falcon.

GOLDFISH IS HUNGRY!

(This is not a code.)

And he ran downstairs to help feed his and Eleanor's kitten.

About the author:

In addition to *Owen and Eleanor Move In*, **H.M. Bouwman** writes middle grade historical fantasy, including *The Remarkable & Very True Story of Lucy & Snowcap* (2008) and *A Crack in the Sea* (2017). She is also an associate professor of English at the University of St. Thomas, a homeschooling mom, a member of Hamline United Methodist Church, and a martial artist.

About the illustrator:

Charlie Alder has illustrated many books for children, including her first authored and illustrated picture book, *Daredevil Duck* (2015). She describes herself as "a curly haired coffee drinker and crayon collector." She lives in Devon, England, with her husband and son.

Coming Fall 2018

Owen is doing the same creative writing project for homeschooling that Eleanor is doing in public school! They have to write an interesting story about their lives. The problem is: their lives aren't that interesting. So Eleanor decides to fix the problem by doing exciting things--with not-so-great results. When they join a community martial arts class, Owen sees a different way to make an interesting story happen... by making something up that sounds true even though it isn't. When they both end up in trouble—again—they learn that making up fake stories to fool people isn't a good way to live.

ISBN: 978-1-5064-4845-9